GOSCINNY AND UDERZO
PRESENT
ASTERIX ADVENTURE

ASTERIX AND THE
MAGIC CARPET

WRITTEN AND ILLUSTRATED BY UDERZO
TRANSLATED BY ANTHEA BELL AND DEREK HOCKRIDGE

British Library Cataloguing in Publication Data

Goscinny, *1926–1977*
  Asterix and the magic carpet
  I. Title   II. Uderzo   III. [Asterix chez Rahazade, *English*]
  843.914[J]

  ISBN 0 340 53339 0

Original edition © Les Editions Albert René, Goscinny-Uderzo, 1987
English Translation © Les Editions Albert René, Goscinny-Uderzo, 1988
Exclusive licensee: Hodder and Stoughton Ltd
Translators: Anthea Bell and Derek Hockridge

First published in Great Britain 1988 (cased)
by Hodder and Stoughton Children's Books
This edition first published 1991 by Knight Books

10 9 8 7 6 5 4

Published by Hodder Children's Books,
a division of Hodder Headline plc
338 Euston Road, London, NW1 3BH

Printed in Belgium by Proost International Book Production

GOSCINNYRIX   VDERZORIX

VIS COMICA★

★ The power to make people laugh: from an epigram by Caesar on Terence, the Latin poet.

The year is 50 BC. Gaul is entirely occupied by the Romans. Well, not entirely... One small village of indomitable Gauls still holds out against the invaders. And life is not easy for the Roman legionaries who garrison the fortified camps of Totorum, Aquarium, Laudanum and Compendium...

OH, WHAT A BEAUTIFUL MORNING, OH, WHAT A BEAUTIFUL DAY... AND THE GAULS HAVE GOT A WONDERFUL FEELING EVERYTHING'S GOING THEIR WAY IN THEIR BRAND-NEW VILLAGE...

FOR AS YOU MAY REMEMBER...

THE ROMANS BURNED OUR VILLAGE TO THE GROUND*. CAESAR, ASHAMED OF WHAT THEY HAD DONE, TOLD HIS MEN TO REBUILD IT...FAIR ENOUGH, BUT THAT DOESN'T MEAN WE'RE ALL SQUARE. AND SO, DEAR FRIENDS...

*SEE ASTERIX AND SON

...I PROPOSE A TOAST TO THE REBIRTH OF THIS IMPOSING AND MAGNIFICENT SYMBOL OF OUR RESISTANCE TO THE ROMAN EMPIRE, AND IN PAYING SUITABLE TRIBUTE TO THIS, THE LAST BULWARK OF THE LIBERTIES OF OUR GREAT GAULISH NATION, I SAY TO YOU NOW...

I REALLY LIKED WATCHING THE ROMANS REBUILD OUR VILLAGE, ASTERIX!

YES, SPECIALLY WHEN THEY WERE GOING SLOW AND YOU THREW MENHIRS AT THEM TO SHOW YOU COULD STONEWALL TOO!

...I SAY TO YOU NOW...

WELL, THEY DID GET THE JOB DONE AHEAD OF SCHEDULE!

FEAR IS SOMETIMES A REMARKABLE STIMULUS, OBELIX!

HOW NICE TO HAVE BRAND-NEW HUTS TO LIVE IN!

YES, BUT I WOULDN'T HAVE MINDED A SPOT OF MODERN ARCHITECTURE WHILE THEY WERE ABOUT IT. FOR INSTANCE, VILLAS IN THE GALLO-ROMAN STYLE!

ROMAN COLUMNS ARE A TERRIBLE PRICE... SIMPLY RUINOUS!

THAT'S FUNNY...I DON'T SEEM TO SEE CACOFONIX THE BARD ANYWHERE!

5

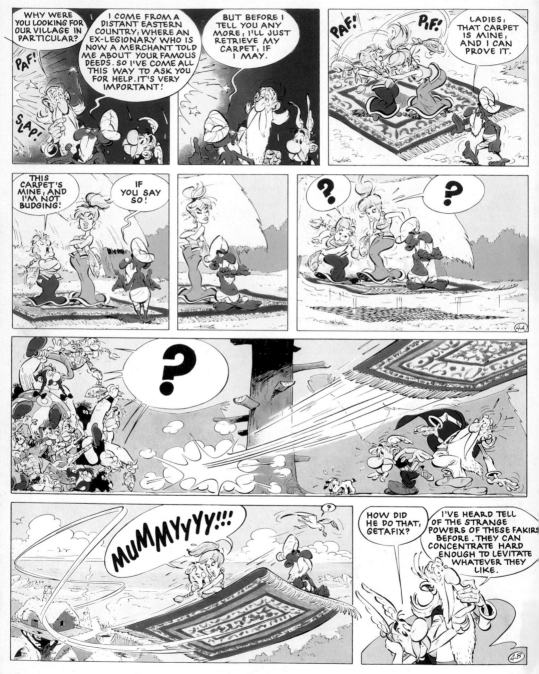

9

11

12

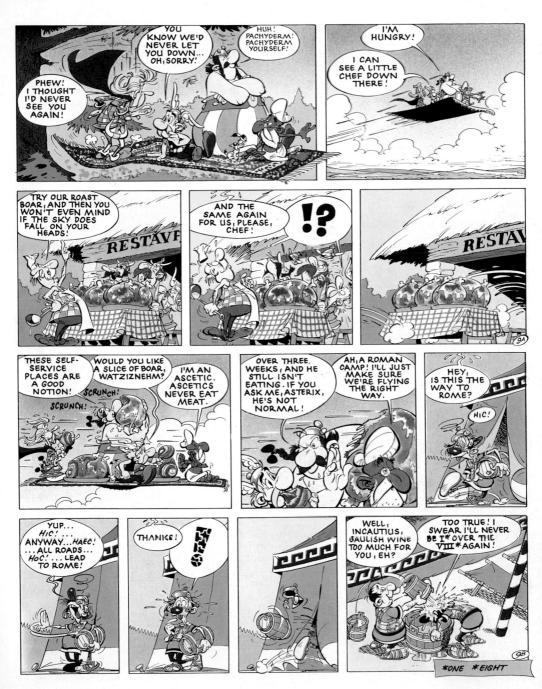

13

14

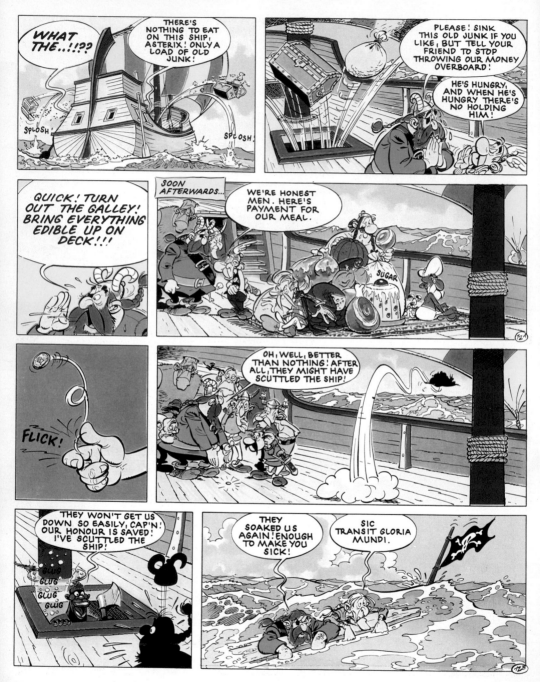

16

21

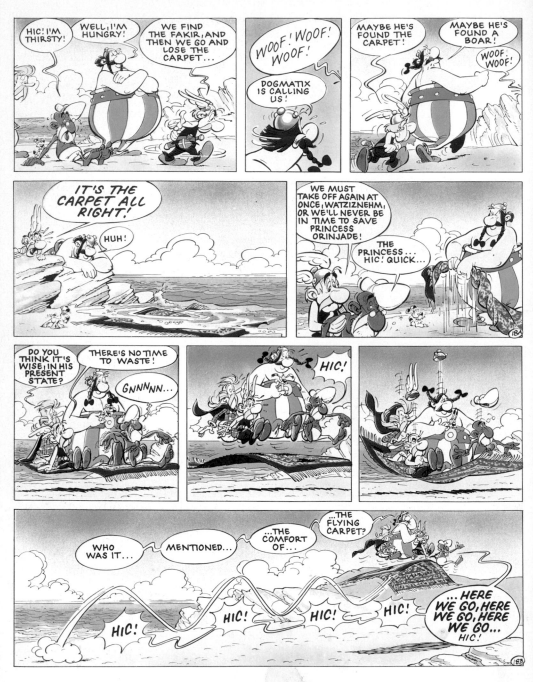

22

26

27

31

33

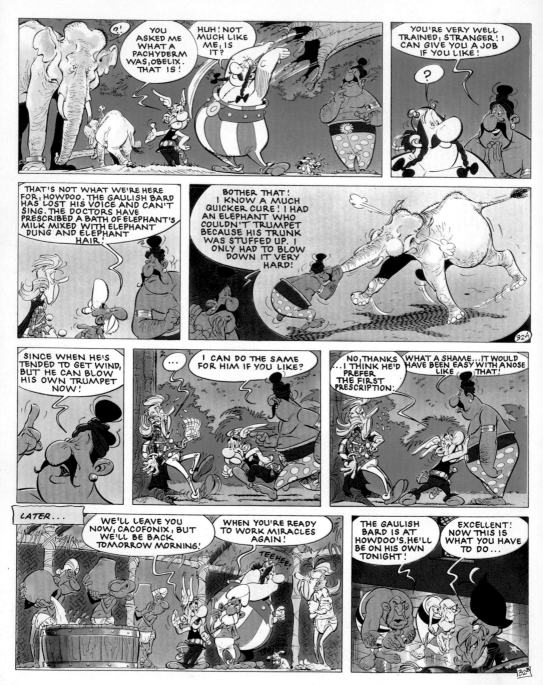

41

44